P9-DBO-972

Etta Can Get It!

FOLLETT DOUBLE SCOOP BOOKS

The Troll Family Stories

- Hi, Dog!
- A Dog Is Not a Troll
- Go, Wendall, Go!
- I Love Wheels
- Etta Can Get It!
- A Troll, a Truck, and a Cookie

Other series of Follett Double Scoop Books:

The Cora Cow Tales

The Adventures of Pippin

Etta Can Get It!

Phylliss Adams
Eleanore Hartson
Mark Taylor

Illustrated by Dennis Hockerman

Follett Publishing Company
Chicago, Illinois
Atlanta, Georgia • Dallas, Texas
Sacramento, California • Warrensburg, Missouri

Text copyright © 1982 by Phylliss Adams, Eleanore Hartson, and Mark Taylor. Illustrations and cover design copyright © 1982 by Follett Publishing Company, a division of Follett Corporation. All rights reserved. No portion of this book may be reproduced in any form without written permission from the publisher. Manufactured in the United States of America.

LC 81-17410
ISBN 0-695-41616-2
ISBN 0-695-31616-8 (pbk.)

"Look," said Wendall.
"We have to get money."

"Money?" said Blossom and Buddy.

"Money," said Leona.
"We have to get money."

"I can get it," said Etta.
"I can get money."

"Come with me," said Etta.
"I can work to make money.
You can help me with my work."

"Get to work," said Etta.
"We can make money."

"I love it," said Blossom.

"Money, money, money!" said Buddy.

"Here we go," said Etta.
"Work, work, work."

Etta's
Car
Wash

"We have to work for money,"
said Buddy.
"We can help you."

B4-621

"See here," said Wendall.
"This is not funny!
You can not get money for this."

"Come with me," said Etta.
"I can work to make money.
You can help me with my work."

Etta's
Lawn
Service

"I love this work," said Blossom.

"It is play to me," said Buddy.

"I love money," said Etta.
"I love to work for money."

"This is not funny!" said Buddy.
"We can not get money for this."

Etta said, "Come with me.
I can make money.
And you can help me make it."

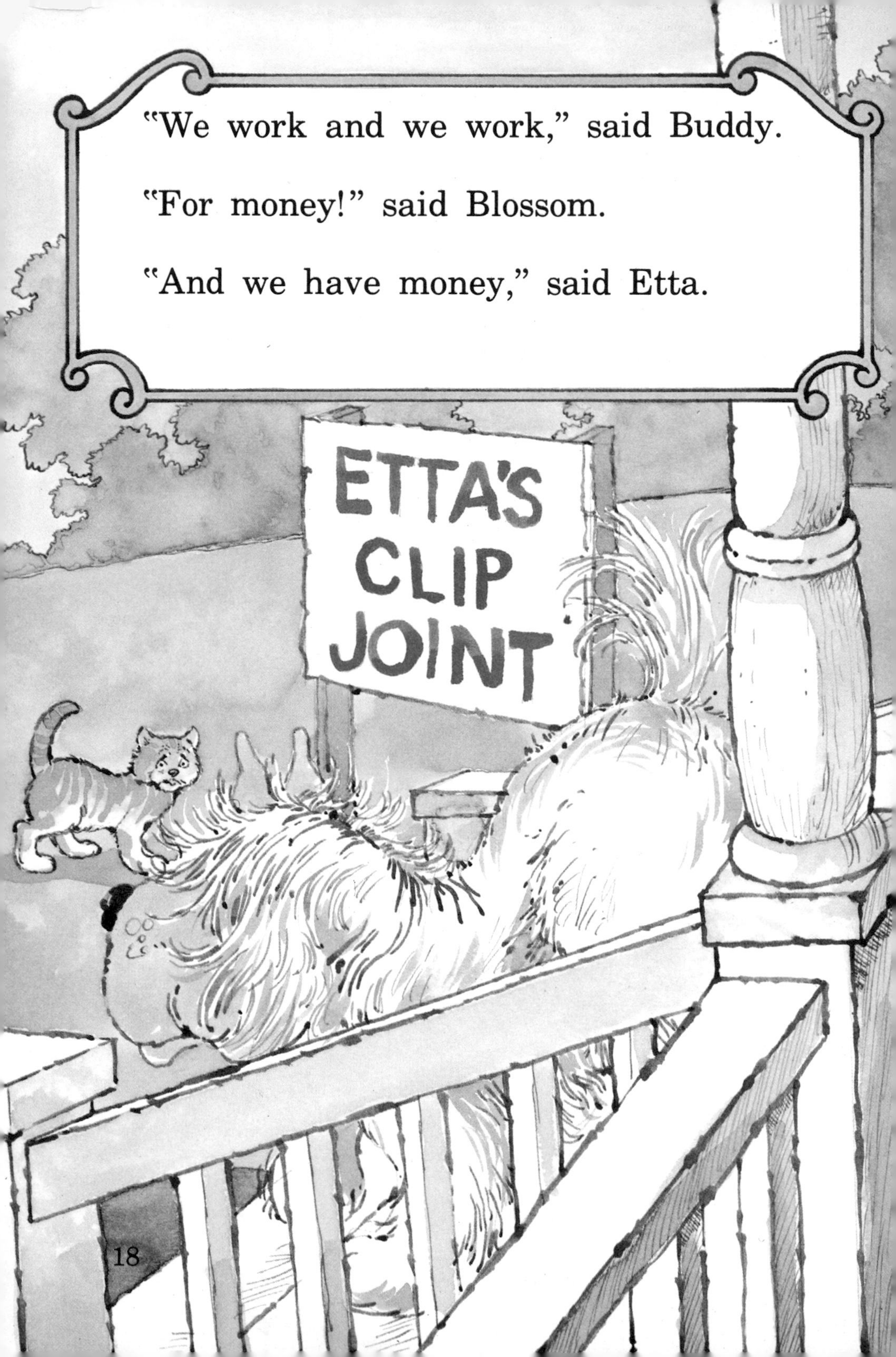
"We work and we work," said Buddy.
"For money!" said Blossom.
"And we have money," said Etta.
ETTA'S
CLIP
JOINT

"Look," said Wendall.
"This is not funny!
You can not get money for this."

Etta said, "Come with me.
We have to have money.
And I can get it."

"We love to work," said Etta.
"We love to play.
And Dandy Dog is funny.
We can make money!"

"We have money," said Wendall.

"We love money," said Blossom.

"And I can get it!" said Etta.

The Troll Word Book

get Dandy Dog can get a ride.

help Buddy can help with the work.

make Blossom can help make money.

If necessary, read these directions to the child:
Read the words and sentences.

me — This cake is for me.

my — This is my balloon.

with — Come with me.

Funny Work

Find the funny things in the picture.

Riddle Fun

Read the riddles and try to guess the answers.
Turn the book upside down to see if your answers are right.

It can come down.
It can not go up.

rain

You can see it.
It can not see you.

turtle

You can ride it.
It can not go.

toy horse

It is for play.
It is not funny.

football

It can go up and up.
It is not a balloon.

helicopter

Etta Can Get It! is the fifth book of the Troll Family Stories for beginning readers. All words used in the story are listed here. (The words in darker print were introduced in this book. The other words were introduced in earlier books.)

and
Blossom
Buddy
can
come
Dandy Dog
Etta

for
funny
get
go
have
help
here
I
is
it

Leona
look
love
make
me
money
my
not
play

said
see
this
to
we
Wendall
with
work
you

About the Authors

Phylliss Adams, Eleanore Hartson, and Mark Taylor have a combined background that includes writing books for children and teachers, teaching at the elementary and university levels, and working in the areas of curriculum development, reading instruction and research, teacher training, parent education, and library and media services.

About the Illustrator

Since his graduation from Layton School of Art in Milwaukee, Wisconsin, Dennis Hockerman has concentrated primarily on art for children's books, magazines, greeting cards, and games.

The artist lives and works in his home in Mequon, Wisconsin, with his wife and two children. The children enjoyed many hours in their dad's studio watching as the Troll Family characters came to life.

123456789/8685848382